Samuel French Acting Edition

I0591734

Howard Crabtree's When Pigs Fly

Conceived by
Howard Crabtree
& Mark Waldrop

Sketches and lyrics by
Mark Waldrop

Music by
Dick Gallagher

FOR PRODUCTION ENQUIRIES

UNITED STATES AND CANADA
info@concordtheatricals.com
1-866-979-0447

UNITED KINGDOM AND EUROPE
licensing@concordtheatricals.co.uk
020-7054-7200

Each title is subject to availability from Concord Theatricals Corp., depending upon country of performance. Please be aware that *WHEN PIGS FLY* may not be licensed by Concord Theatricals Corp. in your territory. Professional and amateur producers should contact the nearest Concord Theatricals Corp. office or licensing partner to verify availability.

be invented, including mechanical, electronic, photocopying, recording, videotaping, or otherwise, without the prior written permission of the publisher. No one shall upload this title(s), or part of this title(s), to any social media websites.

For all enquiries regarding motion picture, television, and other media rights, please contact Concord Theatricals Corp.

MUSIC USE NOTE

Licensees are solely responsible for obtaining formal written permission from copyright owners to use copyrighted music in the performance of this play and are strongly cautioned to do so. If no such permission is obtained by the licensee, then the licensee must use only original music that the licensee owns and controls. Licensees are solely responsible and liable for all music clearances and shall indemnify the copyright owners of the play(s) and their licensing agent, Concord Theatricals Corp., against any costs, expenses, losses and liabilities arising from the use of music by licensees. Please contact the appropriate music licensing authority in your territory for the rights to any incidental music.

IMPORTANT BILLING AND CREDIT REQUIREMENTS

If you have obtained performance rights to this title, please refer to your licensing agreement for important billing and credit requirements.

WHEN PIGS FLY was first produced by Gail Homer Seay, Peter Hauser, and Jane M. Abernethy in association with Mark Howard Segan at the Douglas Fairbanks Theater under the direction of Eric Krebs in New York, New York on August 14, 1996. The performance was directed by Mark Waldrop, with sets and lights by Peter Hauser, sound by Rob Gorton, costumes by Howard Crabtree, and musical direction by Philip Fortenberry. The production stage manager was Glynn David Turner. The cast was as follows:

STANLEY BOJARSKI
JOHN TREACY EGAN
DAVID PEVSNER
JAY ROGERS
MICHAEL WEST
KEITH CROMWELL (UNDERSTUDY)

A revised and updated version was presented as a benefit for The Actors Fund at the Gerald Lynch Theatre at John Jay College in New York, New York on April 9, 2018 with the following cast:

JORDAN AHNQUIST
TAYLOR CROUSORE
JACOB HOFFMAN
FRANK VIVEROS
BRIAN CHARLES ROONEY

CHARACTERS

BRIAN
JACOB
TAYLOR
FRANK
HOWARD

A NOTE FROM MARK WALDROP

If you're getting ready to present *Howard Crabtree's When Pigs Fly* – and I hope you are – there's one word I want you to remember as you're putting it together and performing it: INNOCENCE. There's a sweetness that should permeate this show that might at first seem at odds with its gay themed, cross dressing, double-entendre laced content. But that's the chemistry that makes the show work.

Howard has no agenda. He is an innocent joyfully pursuing his dream. It never occurs to him that anyone would object to his putting on feathers and lashes. In Howard's world the audience's acceptance and delight are a given. This cheery outlook extends to all the Dream Curlys who populate the stage. There is no '90s in-your-face drag attitude here – only the giddy exhilaration that comes with permission to put on a costume and become anything – a mermaid, a playing card, a centaur, a cowboy, a character from a '60s sitcom, a showgirl, a pig – *anything* that will serve a s springboard into laughter.

The heart of *When Pigs Fly* is its through-line, the thread on which the rest of the show is hung. Granted, this is a revue – but as Carol Ann wisely notes, audiences like a story with their music. The story here centers on Howard's mounting anxiety as he confronts the setbacks brought on by his oversized vision and battles self-doubt as personified by Miss Roundhole. Even within the show's broad semi-burlesque style, these scenes must be played honestly, with a sense of urgency and high stakes. The more seriously Howard takes his struggle, the funnier it is – and the more surprised and moved the audience will be by the genuine emotional payoff at the end of the show.

In your production the cast members should be called by their own names – with the exception of Howard, who is always Howard.

Finally, a word about the words – there are lots of them here. These lyrics have points to make and jokes to land. Audiences are not used to listening as actively as they must to fully enjoy these songs. You have to clue them in right from the top that they'll be rewarded for tuning in to the words. Serve the lyrics up. Relish them. Enunciate. Don't take the tempos too fast. Don't let the accompaniment overbalance the singers. Don't let the staging pull focus on the punchlines. Combining all these techniques will help you get full value from the material.

Now, crank up your creativity, shift your sense of humor into high gear, and have a ball.

NOTE ABOUT UPDATES

The author is open to providing updates to the topical parts of *When Pigs Fly*, namely the three "Torch Songs." Please contact your Concord Theatricals licensing representative if you have specific ideas about updates for those songs in your production.

SONG LIST

ACT I

"When Pigs Fly".. Company
"Stay in the Game"................... Brian, Frank, Taylor & Howard
"Torch Song – Part 1: 'Don'".................................. Jacob
"Mermaid Crossover" ....Brian
"Light in the Loafers" .... Frank & Taylor
"Coming Attractions" .... Frank, Jacob, Brian & Taylor
"Pizza Boy" .... Howard
"Carol Ann Finale"........................... Brian, Jacob & Frank
"Not All Man"... Taylor
"Torch Song – Part 2: 'Mike'"................................. Jacob
"Garden of Eden"................................... Taylor & Brian
"Color Out of Colorado" .... Company

ACT II

"Wear Your Vanity With Pride"............................. Company
"Last One Picked" .... Howard
"The Nerd" .... Jacob
"Freak" .... Frank, Brian & Howard
"Sam and Me"...................................... Taylor & Brian
"Bigger is Better" .... Frank
"Torch Song – Part 3: 'Vlad'"................................. Jacob
"Laughing Matters".. Jacob
"Over the Top" .... Howard & Company

ACT I

(The set is an old-fashioned vaudeville stage that has seen better days. Parts of the proscenium ornamentation are broken or missing. Plaster and lath peek through in spots. Filling the proscenium opening is a once rich Austrian drape, now threadbare. There is a curtained pass door stage left. Apparently some kind of renovation has been underway, because there is scaffolding stage right holding an array of paint cans, drop cloths and plastic tubs of joint compound on platforms at different levels. In amongst the scaffolding are a piano and a drum kit. The **PIANIST** *and* **DRUMMER** *enter and take their places. House lights dim. The stage lights blush up. What looked vaguely haunted in pre-set now looks warm and inviting.)*

HOWARD. *(Voice over.)* Hello, everybody! The management has asked me to announce that the use of recording devices or cameras is strictly prohibited by law! Thanks, and enjoy the show...

[MUSIC NO. 01 "WHEN PIGS FLY – OPENING"]

Hey! I bet all of you are thinking – *When Pigs Fly*?! How'd they ever come up with *that* title?

(House lights out.)

(Underscoring continues.)

Well, let me explain. It all started one fateful afternoon when I was in high school.

(The Austrian drape rises.)

I can see it just like it was yesterday...yesterday...yesterday...

PROLOGUE

(A banner hangs mid-stage. On it: "SPRINGBROOK HIGH SCHOOL. 1992." There's a two-dimensional desk stage right with a name-plate reading "MISS ROUNDHOLE." At center, facing upstage, is **MISS ROUNDHOLE** *herself. Clipboard in hand, she turns, glances at her wristwatch, crosses to the desk, leans into a desk microphone and speaks. Through the school's sound system we hear...)*

MISS ROUNDHOLE. *(Voice over.)* Howard Crabtree! You are late for your three o'clock appointment. Howard Crabtree, please report to the guidance counselor.

> **(HOWARD** *enters, a high school senior; bursting with sweetness and enthusiasm. He's in crudely glamorized western gear: a ten gallon hat, chaps, the works – decorated with ric-rac and sparkle paints.)*

HOWARD. Sorry I'm late, Miss Roundhole. I was at play practice.

MISS ROUNDHOLE. Howard Crabtree! What is this get-up you're wearing?

HOWARD. Do you like it? I made it myself!

MISS ROUNDHOLE. And just what are you supposed to be?

HOWARD. Dream Curly.

MISS ROUNDHOLE. Since when does Dream Curly wear feather chaps, a sparkle vest, and false eyelashes?!

3

HOWARD. I guess it depends on who's dreaming.

MISS ROUNDHOLE. Never mind! We're here to review your vocational test. I have to say; I couldn't make head or tail of it. Like here: Career Goal! You're supposed to pick one of the *pre-printed* answers, not write something in!

HOWARD. But you didn't have my career goal on the list...

MISS ROUNDHOLE. Being an "Ice Capade" is not a career goal! Wake up and smell the Sanka! This is Missouri, Howard. Now, I've narrowed your options down to four:

[MUSIC NO. 02 "WHEN PIGS FLY"]

Watch Repair. Garden Supply. Plumbing. Chicken Farming.

HOWARD. But I'd be bored doing those jobs...

MISS ROUNDHOLE. Making a living isn't supposed to be fun. That's why it's called work.

HOWARD. But I want to put on shows! Sing and dance and make funny costumes!

MISS ROUNDHOLE. And sell the tickets and pop the popcorn, right?

HOWARD. Sure! And I'll find other people to help me! People who feel the same way I do! People like me!

MISS ROUNDHOLE. People like you are just going through a stage!

HOWARD. No, wait, Miss Roundhole! Can't you see it? Me and all the other Dream Curlys from all the other high schools all over the country-putting on a show! A show where we play all the parts, we sing the big torch songs, we have all the good jokes! Can't you see it, Miss Roundhole?

MISS ROUNDHOLE. Well, when you put it that way, Howard, sure. I can see it... WHEN PIGS FLY!!!

(Lights momentarily zoom in to a pin-spot on HOWARD's face. Psycho nightmare piano chords. Then the lights bump up. HOWARD steps out of the flashback. The opening number kicks in.)

HOWARD.
WELL, MISS ROUNDHOLE, THE JIG IS UP. THE PIG IS UP IN THE AIR.
I'M COMIN' THROUGH, THE COAST IS CLEAR:
BE GONE! YOU HAVE NO POWER HERE...

(As the desk rolls off stage right, HOWARD yanks the banner down, wraps it around MISS ROUNDHOLE – who is agreeably mortified – and propels her into the wings. HOWARD addresses the audience.)

TONIGHT WE'RE STAGING A GRAND REVUE,
AND IT'S NOT JUST A STAGE WE'RE GOING THROUGH!

Ladies and gentlemen, please <u>un</u>fasten your safety belts and prepare for take-off!

WHEN PIGS FLY
EV'RY RULE IS SUSPENDED! WHEN PIGS FLY
COMMON SENSE IS UP-ENDED!
SO TAKE A SEAT AND SETTLE BACK.
IT'S A MAJOR AIRBORNE PORK ATTACK!
WHEN PIGS FLY
POSSIBILITY BECKONS.
NO ALTERNATE SIDE OF THE BRAIN RESTRICTIONS APPLY!
BROTHER, YOU AIN'T SEEN A THING TILL YOU'VE SEEN BACON TAKIN' WING! WHEN PIGS FLY!

(During Chorus two, four more pastel costumed Dream Curlys – BRIAN, JACOB, FRANK, and TAYLOR – enter and join in.)

WHEN PIGS FLY

ALL.

> INHIBITIONS HAVE VANISHED!
> WHEN PIGS FLY
> REGULATIONS ARE BANISHED!
> SO JUST RELAX, ENJOY THE SHOW!
> IT'S OINKERS UP AND AWAY WE GO!
> WHEN PIGS FLY
> THE BLUE YONDER GETS WILDER.
> IT'S TOO LATE TO CANCEL THE TRIP, SO DON'T EVEN TRY!
> TAKE A LOOK AND YOU MIGHT SPY ARNOLD ZIFFEL
>   ZOOMING BY
> WHEN PIGS FLY!

BRIAN.

> IT'S A TINY EXTRAVAGANZA.

JACOB.

> IT'S A GIANT PERFORMANCE PIECE.

TAYLOR.

> WE'VE GOT GUYS WHO SING LIKE MARIO LANZA

> *(**FRANK** hits a high note.)*

FRANK.

> AHH!
> AND GUYS WHO DANCE LIKE CYD CHARISSE!

> *(**TAYLOR** executes a vampy step.)*

> Not now Taylor, later!

HOWARD.

> IT ISN'T BLOATED LIKE BROADWAY.
> IT ISN'T ARTY LIKE BAM!

ALL.

> IT'S A GREAT BIG PARTY SMORGASBORD.

HOWARD.

> WITH A GENEROUS HELPING OF HAM!

ALL.

WHEN PIGS FLY
LEAVE YOUR GRAVITY EARTHBOUND!
OUR HUMOR IS CERTAINLY LOW, BUT SPIRITS ARE HIGH!

JACOB.

SEE THOSE WEENIES AVIATE!

ALL.

THEY'LL BLAST RIGHT PAST HOG-HEAVEN'S GATE
WHEN PIGS FLY!

> *(Dance break.)*

WINGS!!

> *(They pick up flashlights tipped with red cones. Lights dim as they do some Busby Berkley-style landing crew choreography.)*

OOOOH!
AAUGHHHHH!

> *(Lights restore. **HOWARD** exits.)*

QUARTET.

WHEN PIGS FLY
GRAB YOUR OVER-THE-TOP HAT!
WE'RE DRESSED FOR EXCESS, THE LIMIT'S ONLY THE SKY!
THE SHOW'S A QUEER ONE, THERE'S NO DOUBT:
JUST TO BE IN IT, YOU GOT TO BE OUT!
SO KISS YOUR DISAPPOINTMENTS ALL GOOD-BYE!

> *(**HOWARD** re-enters in a much dreamier Dream Curly costume.)*

HOWARD.

SWINE SWIRLS AROUND LIKE WHIRLIGIGS,
FLAPPIN' WINGS AND FLIPPIN' WIGS

ALL.

WHEN PIGS... WHEN PIGS FLY! OINK!

(Applause. **HOWARD** *steps downstage and the curtain falls behind him.)*

[MUSIC NO. 03 "PIGS PLAYOFF"]

("Crossover #1.")

HOWARD. Thank you, ladies and gentlemen, and *welcome*! I'm thrilled you could be here tonight for this – the show I've always dreamed of doing! We've got fabulous songs, queer-ball sketches, gags 'n' gimmicks galore – all served up by some of the best talent in town! Just like *New Faces of 1952* introduced Paul Lynde, Eartha Kitt, and Carol Lawrence, we'll be introducing you to some of the freshest...

*(***JACOB** *bursts through the pass-door.)*

JACOB. Excuse me – Howard?

HOWARD. Um...what is it, Jacob? ... Jacob Hoffman, ladies and gentlemen.

*(***HOWARD** *leads the applause.)*

JACOB. I hate to interrupt right at the top of the show and everything, but...

*(***JACOB** *whispers into* **HOWARD***'s ear.)*

HOWARD. Oh! Excuse me, ladies and gentlemen. There's a tiny crisis backstage. Nothing to worry about. Jacob, would you introduce the next number?

*(***HOWARD** *rushes off.)*

JACOB. Of course, Howard. *(To the audience.)* It's really not a crisis. It's just Taylor – you know, that well-built boy with all the animal magnetism? Did you spot him in the opening number? Mmmm-hmmm. Well, he had a little quick-change mishap. Now he needs his zipper waxed... Anyway, that's Howard's department. Not only did he *design* all the costumes, he's also the star of the show *and* the wardrobe mistress. He wears so many hats. And they're all so *big*. That's the problem. Howard's put everything he's got into this show. Literally. There isn't room to turn around back there!

(He lowers his voice slightly. This is the real dirt.) Let me explain... All five of us – and the costumes – are squeezed into one tiny dressing room.

And the rest of the backstage is still under "reconstruction" – you know, scaffolding, drop cloths, power tools. Have you noticed that the renovation of the old "Little Shubert" is running behind schedule? You see, Howard was a bit over-optimistic when he set the opening date. Oh, don't get me wrong, it's not that we don't love Howard – he just tends to get a little carried away. And *speaking* of getting carried away, let's see if we're ready to get on with the show...

> *(He peeks through the pass door and stifles a laugh.)*

Oh, brother. And you thought I was a big queen... Wait till you see what we have in store for you. Ladies and gentlemen, without further ado, the Casino Sisters...

> *(**JACOB** exits through the pass-door as the curtain rises.)*

[MUSIC NO. 04 "YOU'VE GOT TO STAY IN THE GAME"]

> *(**FOUR QUEENS** are revealed. With their stylized two-dimensional costumes- individually emblazoned with hearts, diamonds, club, and spades – they might have stepped right out of a deck of cards. Their vocal style could be described as the Boswell Sisters meet Kay Thompson...)*

QUEEN OF SPADES (HOWARD).
>YOUR HOUSE OF CARDS HAS FALLEN FLAT.
>ROMANCE IS OUT THE DOOR.

QUEEN OF HEARTS (TAYLOR).
>YOU SHAKE YOUR HEAD AND ASK YOURSELF,

QUEEN OF CLUBS (FRANK).
>"WHAT DO I NEED THIS FOR?"

QUEEN OF DIAMONDS (BRIAN).
>YOUR FINGER WITH NO DIAMOND.

QUEEN OF HEARTS.
>YOUR HEART WORN TO A NUB.

QUEEN OF SPADES.
>YOU'VE LEARNED YOUR LESSON,

ALL.
>YES, IN SPADES.

QUEEN OF CLUBS.
>WELL, HONEY, WELCOME TO THE CLUB!

ALL.
>BUT DON'T GET UP FROM WHERE YOU SIT –
>REMEMBER, WINNERS NEVER QUIT.
>STICK IT OUT FOR ONE MORE ROUND,
>'CAUSE FROM PERSONAL EXPERIENCE WE HAVE FOUND...
>IF YOU WANT TO WIN AT LOVE
>YOU'VE GOT TO STAY IN THE GAME.
>PULLIN' OUT WHILE YOU'RE BEHIND
>WOULD BE A DOGGONE CRYIN' SHAME.
>JUST RE-SHUFFLE, CUT THE DECK.
>WHO KNOWS? MAYBE SOON (MAYBE SOON).
>YOU COULD HOLD A LUCKY HAND
>AND BABY – YOU COULD SHOOT THE MOON!
>YOUR LOSIN' STREAK'S GONNA HAVE A HICCUP.
>IT COULD BE THE NEXT TRICK YOU PICK UP!
>IF YOU WANT TO WIN AT LOVE

YOU'VE GOT TO STAY IN THE GAME!

IF YOU WANT TO WIN AT LOVE,
YOU'VE GOT TO STAY IN THE GAME.
THIS COULD BE THE ONE YOU ACE!
LADY LUCK IS A CHANGEABLE DAME!
MR. RIGHT IS WAITING
SOMEWHERE IN THE PACK.

IF SHE HANGS ON LONG ENOUGH, A QUEEN WILL ALWAYS
TAKE A JACK!
BIDE YOUR TIME AND WAIT A WHILE.
DON'T WIND UP IN THE DISCARD PILE!
IF YOU WANT TO WIN AT LOVE
YOU'VE GOT TO STAY IN THE GAME.

Bridge!

BLACKJACK, BACCARAT, GIN, SPITE AND MALICE,
GO FISHHH! EUCHRE AND CANASTA,
WHISSSSST, PINOCHLE, A-FIVE A-CARD, A-FIVE CARD
    STUD!
WHOOPS! STRIP POKER, RUMMY, THREE-CARD-MONTE,
SPIT! WAR! FIFTY-TWO PICK-UP!
FAN-TAN! CRAZY EIGHTS!
OLD MAID? SOLITAIRE? OH, NO, NO, NO!

IF YOU WANT TO WIN AT LOVE,
YOU'VE GOT TO STAY IN THE GAME.
ALL IT TAKES IS ONE GRAND SLAM –
LIFE'LL NEVER BE THE SAME!
WE HAVE JUST ONE SAFETY TIP
THAT SHOULD BE DULY NOTED:
BEFORE YOU GET YOUR ANTE UP
MAKE SURE THOSE CARDS ARE PLASTIC COATED!
THE TURNAROUND JUST TAKES A MINUTE.
ON THIS DEAL YOU'RE BOUND TO WIN IT!
BUT YOU'VE GOT TO PLAY,
BABY, THAT'S THE ONLY WAY! HEY!
YOU'VE GOT TO STAY IN THE GAME!

STAY IN THE GAME!
STAY IN THE GAME!
YOU'VE GOT TO STAY IN THE GAME!

[MUSIC NO. 04A "STAY IN THE GAME PLAYOFF"]

(Curtain.)

[MUSIC NO. 05 "TORCH SONG – PART 1: 'DON'"]

(JACOB, in a dinner jacket, drags on a chair through the pass-door. He crosses to stage right, sets the chair and drapes himself across it elegantly. From his pocket he produces a pink chiffon scarf. We're about to hear a torch song.)

JACOB.
EV'RYONE I LOVE IS ALWAYS, ALWAYS
UNATTAINABLE.
WHY DO I WANT WHAT I CAN'T HAVE?
IT'S UNEXPLAINABLE.
I KNOW I OUGHT TO TURN
AND RUN THE OTHER WAY,
BUT EXCUSE ME, DONALD TRUMP –
THERE'S SOMETHING I MUST SAY...
DON...
OH, YES, WE'RE ON.
YOU SCHLUMPY, DUMPY... HUMPY... PUTIN PAWN.
I'M ALL A-TWITTER
AND SO BESOTTED
I TREASURE EVERY IDIOTIC
TWEET YOU'VE TWATTED.
DON
MY PRIDE IS GONE
ALL MY PAST OBJECTIONS ARE WITHDRAWN!

I ADORE THOSE GREAT BIG TOWERS
THAT YOU BUILT YOUR FAME ON.
NOW I'M ERECTING SOMETHING
YOU CAN PUT YOUR NAME ON.

DON

SO PUT UPON!

HEY, FUCK THOSE UGLY DUCKLINGS, YOU'RE A SWAN!!
WHILE YOU LAY WASTE TO THIS GREAT NATION
I'LL CATER TO YOUR SIZE FIXATION –
I'LL CALL THAT... BABY SHRIMP A JUMBO PRAWN!

BUT THAT'S PIE IN THE SKY
WHEN YOU CARRY A TORCH FOR A GUY
LIKE MY MAN...

DON.

> *(Blackout.)*

[MUSIC NO. 06 "MERMAID CROSSOVER"]

> *(Ethereal music. The curtain rises. A bare breasted* **MERMAID** *is revealed, posed on a conch shell. Her clouds of billowing blue hair waft upward, creating a seaweed-like effect.)*

MERMAID (BRIAN).

THERE'S A WRECK AT THE BOTTOM OF THE SEA,
WHERE THE EAST IS EAST AND THE WEST IS WEST.
HANDSOME TREASURE SEEKER, COME TO ME,
AND YOU WILL FIND A SUNKEN CHEST.
OH.
WITH A BLOW ME HIGH AND A BLOW ME LOW,
AND A BLOW ME DOWN IN THE BRINY DEEP,
WITH A HA-HA HERE, AND A HO-HO THERE...

> *(Something is wrong. The* **MERMAID** *stops the song.)*

BRIAN. Wait a minute! Wait a minute! Hey! Where's the treasure chest? Where's the pirate ship? This is unbelievable!

> (**BRIAN** *ducks out of the* **MERMAID** *wig, which remains dangling. Lights change; the glamorous illusion is shattered.* **BRIAN** *moves downstage. He is now a cranky man in a wig cap and bare breasted mermaid suit.*)

Howard! Could you come out here please?

> (**HOWARD** *rushes on looking a bit frazzled.*)

HOWARD. Brian, we'll have the scenery out here in just a minute.

BRIAN. Howard, I am out here trying to give this show some much-needed class.

> (*The audience presumably reacts to this.* **BRIAN** *graciously acknowledges them.*)

Thank you. (*Back to* **HOWARD**.) ...But I cannot work this way. The number makes absolutely no sense without the set. Where is the Pirate Ship?

HOWARD. It's stuck.

BRIAN. The Pirate Ship is stuck?

HOWARD. It's just that much too big. It won't turn around the corner.

BRIAN. Can you back it up and try again?

HOWARD. It's really kind of wedged in...

> (**FRANK** *leans on from between the proscenium and the curtain.*)

FRANK. Howard! I think we've got it figured out. Those workmen left some power tools...

> (*Buzz saw sound effects.*)

HOWARD. No, wait...! Tell them not to cut the ship...!

(FRANK *retreats to relay the message...too late.* BRIAN *is furious.*)

BRIAN. Well, now that you've had to cut the Mermaid number – literally – that means there's a big hole in the show. What do you want to do, Howard?

(*Lights zoom in to a pin spot on* HOWARD's *face. Psycho nightmare piano chords.*)

MISS ROUNDHOLE. *(Voice over.)* Have you thought about *watch repair*?!!

(*Lights and sound restore.*)

BRIAN. Howard, are you okay?

HOWARD. Yeah. Sorry. I guess we'll have to skip to the next number.

BRIAN. Oh great. Jacob gets to do his solo... Okay – fine! I'll let it go. But I'm telling you right now, that finale thing is not gonna fly!

HOWARD. Brian, we've been through all this before. You have to do the finale.

BRIAN. No! Not in that outfit...

HOWARD. But it's the title of the show.

BRIAN. Howard, I have my pride.

(*The audience presumably reacts to this.* BRIAN *turns on them.*)

...Well, I *do*!

HOWARD. All right, Brian. I understand. How about if we lose the rocket pack?

BRIAN. That would be a start.

HOWARD. Good. If you'll introduce the next number, I'll start snipping those wires.

BRIAN. Thank you.

> (HOWARD *exits*. BRIAN *assumes a suave announcer persona at completely odds with his appearance.*)

And now, ladies and gentlemen, *When Pigs Fly* takes pride in presenting a rather unconventional remedy for an all too common foot problem. Take it away, boys! ...Watch it! Big tail comin' through!

> (BRIAN *exits through the pass door.*)

[MUSIC NO. 07 "LIGHT IN THE LOAFERS"]

> (*The curtain rises. In front of a blue cyclorama,* FRANK *and* TAYLOR *enter gotten up as a couple of vaudevillians – song-and-dance men in matching plaid suits. They do simple rhythmic choreography.*)

FRANK & TAYLOR.
HERE'S THE STORY OF A BROADWAY HOOFER,
AUDITIONED FOR EV'RY SHOW.
HE GOT DOWN TO THE FINAL CUT,
BUT THEN HE GOT THE OLD HEAVE-HO.
ONE DAY HE DIDN'T HEAD FOR HOME,
HE HUNG AROUND INSTEAD.
HE PRESSED HIS EAR UP TO THE DOOR,
AND HERE'S WHAT THOSE PRODUCERS SAID:

FRANK.
"HE'S LIGHT IN THE LOAFERS."

TAYLOR.
"LIGHT IN THE LOAFERS."

FRANK & TAYLOR.
"HE'S LIGHT IN THE LOAFERS.
AND HE AIN'T GONNA GET NO ROLES."
WELL, THAT BROADWAY HOOFER WAS ONE BRIGHT BOY,

HE SAID, "I GOTTA FIGURE OUT
IF TONING DOWN'S THE WAY TO GO,
WHAT BLENDING IN IS ALL ABOUT.
I'VE ALWAYS HEARD, 'JUST BE YOURSELF.'
'TO THINE OWN SELF BE TRUE.'
BUT IF MY FOOTWEAR'S NOT IN STYLE,
SHOULD I PUT MY FOOT IN ANOTHER SHOE?"

IF I'M LIGHT IN THE LOAFERS.
LIGHT IN THE LOAFERS.
IF I'M LIGHT IN THE LOAFERS.
DO I NEED LEAD INNER-SOLES?

FRANK.

BUT SHOULD AN AFRO-AMERICAN, TO REACH HIS GOAL,
TRY TO BE WHITE? SELL HIS SOUL?

TAYLOR.

SHOULD A WOMAN, TO COMPLETE HER PLAN,
HAVE TO MASQUERADE AS A MAN?

FRANK.	**TAYLOR.**
NO!	NO, NO, NO, NO
IF I'M LIGHT IN THE LOAFERS,	NO, NO, NO, NO
LIGHT IN THE LOAFERS,	WHOA, WHOA, WHOA
MR. LIGHT IN THE LOAFERS,	

(Lights in the toes of their shoes come on. They react with surprise and delight.)

THEN I'M GONNA SHINE IT AROUND!

(Dance break. The shoe-lights flash as part of the choreography. They ad-lib. "Light on my feet!" "Shine on my shoes!")

I'M LIGHT-FOOTED, GOODNESS KNOWS!
I PUT A FRESH WRINKLE IN "TWINKLE-TOES"!
I GOTTA SAY, HOW CAN I LOSE

WITH THIS KIND OF SHINE UPON MY SHOES?
YES!

CALL ME LIGHT IN THE LOAFERS,
MR. LIGHT IN THE LOAFERS!
I'LL KEEP MY FEET SIX INCHES OFF THE GROUND!
THEY'RE MEANT FOR MORE THAN PAVEMENT POUNDING.
MY FLASHY FOOTWORK IS ASTOUNDING.
LIGHT IN THE LOAFERS!
LIGHT IN THE LOAFERS!
IF I'M LIGHT IN THE LOAFERS
THEN I'M
GONNA SHINE IT AROUND!
SHINE IT AROUND!

> *(The shoe-lights remain lit just past the blackout.)*

> *("Coming Attractions with Carol Ann.")*

> *(A **WOMAN** enters, clapping, as the applause from the previous number fades. She wears a red, white, and blue nautical outfit. It's impossible to tell her age because she's got so darn much personality – big smile, big eyes, big hair. She's a small town impresario, a 100 Watt bulb in a 60 Watt socket. Curtain lowers behind her.)*

CAROL ANN (BRIAN). We'll be back with the fourth, and final, act of *Anything Goes* as soon as we sell you a few more drinks! And if you need to "stretch your legs," – if you know what I mean – it's through the lobby and to your left.

Now, for those of you who don't know me, I'm Carol Ann Knippel, Artistic Director here at the Melody Barn – and your Reno Sweeny for this evening. But right now what I want to talk to you about is our thrilling plans for next season.

As you know, here at the Melody Barn we are dedicated to bringing you the best of Broadway – shows with zip, zing, and plenty of pizzazz!

Our audience is important to us. That's why we listen to what you want! We know there were some problems with this past season. We know you didn't understand *Fun Home...* And that it wasn't *fun*. We know you don't see why we can't do *Hamilton*. *(An aside.)* I mean, I think it's overrated, but maybe that's me... We know, "Hey, how many times can you *Paint Your Wagon*?!" Message received loud and clear!

So this season we tried changing the pace with some revues. There was our evening of Frank Loesser's World War II songs, *Brutally Frank*. Then there was our Rediscovered Richard Rodgers evening, *You Don't Know Dick*. Hey, they were fun, right? But we know you like a story with your music...

Now what you may *not* know is in recent years the supply of new musicals from Broadway has pretty much dried up. The big hits like *Wicked* keep on running and we can't get the rights to them! *(She expresses her frustration with a little Elphaba riff.)* We can't.

So let's cut to the cheese. The Melody Barn is in a pickle. And, I don't mind telling you, for a while there we all got pretty discouraged. But then I said to myself, Carol Ann! It's time to open a new window! Kiss today good-bye and point me towards tomorrow! Why not write your own darn musicals?! So I put pen to paper and guess what? It's not so hard! In fact it's fun! Just take an old story and pump it full of pep! I enlisted the help of our ever-faithful accompanist, Jason... Jason, take a bow! Hey! Hit him with a spot!

> *(The **PIANIST** has converted himself into **JASON**. He bobs his head in acknowledgment of the applause.)*

He's written all the music, and it's fabulous! Who knew we had a Stephen Sound-heim right under our noses?! That's why all of us here at the Melody Barn are so darn excited! Next season we'll be presenting a whole series of world premiere musicals based on stories that Broadway hasn't gotten around to yet!

And tonight, to boost our subscription program, we're going to show you a few coming attractions! First up, a little song and dance extravaganza we call *Quasimodo! – The Public Domain Musical*! It's the classic love story with a twist. Oh, wait till you see these kids sparkle! Here's the climactic scene. The setting is the top of the bell tower at Notre Dame Cathedral! Down below, the crowd is banging down the church's doors!

[MUSIC NO. 08 "COMING ATTRACTIONS"]

(Curtain rises to reveal **QUASIMODO** *standing at center with* **ESMERELDA** *at his feet. Behind them is a flimsy looking cardboard battlement with holes cut out for the* **GARGOYLES***' faces to come through.)*

QUASIMODO (FRANK). *(Very* Les Mis.*)*
  BONG, BONG, BONG, BONG!
  HARK, ESMERELDA, THE BELLS ARE PEALING:
  BONG, BONG, BONG, BONG!
  SOMEHOW THAT GIVES ME A FUNNY FEELING...

  (Suddenly he's Gene Kelly.)

  NOW I'VE GOT YOU IN MY POWER,
  HIGH ATOP THIS GOTHIC TOWER,
  THERE'S DEATH BELOW AND HEAVEN ABOVE!
  THOUGH THE GATES OF HELL ARE YAWNING,
  STILL I THINK THE TRUTH IS DAWNING:
  I'VE GOT A HUNCH... I'M IN LOVE!

  (The **GARGOYLES** *sing back up.)*

GARGOYLES (HOWARD & TAYLOR).
HE'S GOT A HUNCH! A HUNCH HE'S IN LOVE!
HE'S GOT A HUNCH! A HUNCH HE'S IN LOVE!

> *(***ESMERELDA*** *turns front and holds a Merman-esque "Ah!" through the next section.)*

QUASIMODO.
GO TELL MR. VICTOR HUGO,
KID, WHERE I GO, THAT'S WHERE YOU GO!
WE'RE FLYING ON THE WINGS OF A DOVE!

QUASIMODO & GARGOYLES.
WHAT ABOUT THAT ESMERELDA?

ESMERELDA (JACOB).
I'M A BRASSY BROADWAY BELTAH!

BOTH.
WE'VE GOT A HUNCH... WE'RE IN LOVE!

> *(The curtain falls with a thud.* **CAROL ANN** *leads the applause.)*

CAROL ANN. But wait! There's more. That's just the first show in a season brimming over with excitement and musical comedy know-how! Hey, you never know where you'll find a good story! Jason discovered this one on a video he found under his uncle's bed. And he's written the whole thing! It's all about a group of rowdy frat boys on a ski weekend in a remote mountain cabin. There's a terrible blizzard, and the food they've ordered has just arrived when an avalanche cuts them off from civilization! We call the show... *(She glances at her card.) Falcon Pack 6: Pizza Boy Delivers.* Let's take a peek!

> *(Curtain rises to reveal the* **PIZZA BOY –** **HOWARD** *– in a shaft of light. A gentle snowfall sifts down on him.)*

[MUSIC NO. 08A "PIZZA BOY"]

PIZZA BOY.
THE ROAD GOT BLOCKED, AND I GOT STUCK.
SIX DRUNKEN FRAT BOYS – THEY WERE HUNGRY, TOO.
ONCE THEY POLISHED OFF THAT DOUBLE PEPPERONI,
I SAID, "NOW WHAT DO WE DO?"

THEY SAID, "YOU GOTTA TRY THE HOT TUB,
YOU MUST BE COLD AS ICE!"
SO SOMEONE FIRED UP THE HOT TUB.
WHEN WE GOT IN, IT FELT NICE.
BUT ALL TOO SOON, WE WERE PLOWED OUT.
IT ALMOST SEEMED A SHAME!
THEY SAID, "PIZZA BOY, WE'RE GLAD YOU CAME!"
I SAID, "YOU GUYS – I CAME TWICE."

> *(The curtain falls almost immediately.* **CAROL ANN** *has been peeking through the pass door to make sure her boys are ready for the next number and has missed the last couple of lines. She rushes back to center.)*

CAROL ANN. Oh, I love the ballads… Okay. Last but not least, we've got something I know you're going to love! When we couldn't find a story to suit us, we just took characters whose appeal is tried and true and made up a whole new story around them. I play the title part! So look out! Here comes *Annie 3*!

[MUSIC NOS. 09 & 10 "ANNIE"]

> *(***CAROL ANN*** *exits, almost colliding with a peppy pair of* **CHORUS BOYS** *costumed as butlers who dance on through the pass-door: They perform the traditional double-time rhubarb leading up to a star entrance.)*

CHORUS BOYS (JACOB & FRANK).
WHERE'S THAT GREAT BIG HEIRESS

THAT WE ALL ADORE?
WHERE'S THAT MILLIONAIRESS
WE'VE BEEN WAITING FOR?
SHE USED TO BE AN ORPHAN TYKE,
BUT SHE'S GROWN-UP, AND HOW!
SHE'S A GAL YOU'RE GONNA LIKE,
AND HERE SHE COMES RIGHT NOW!

(The curtain rises on **CAROL ANN,** *breathless from her quick-change, wearing a full length restyling of the classic Annie dress complete with patent leather Mary Janes and anklets. Inexplicably, she's topped off her curly red wig with a* Hello Dolly *feathered head piece.)*

CHORUS BOY #1 (JACOB). Annie! The world's in a mess!

CHORUS BOY #2 (FRANK). Annie! The country's in crisis!

CHORUS BOYS. *(In imperfect unison.)* Annie! As newly appointed head of the president's task force on optimism, what are your plans?

CAROL ANN. First, I'm going to get rid of you two. Bye, bye.

*(***CAROL ANN,** *disgusted, sends them off. The curtain falls. She sings a-la Sophie Tucker.)*

[MUSIC NO. 11 "CAROL ANN FINALE"]

WHEN YOU'RE UP SHIT CREEK WITHOUT A PADDLE,
TELL THOSE PROBLEMS TO SKEDADDLE!
WHEN YOU'RE IN HOT WATER UP TO HERE,
DON'T GO UNDER, PERSEVERE!
LOLLYGAGGERS NEVER WIN!
ROLL UP THOSE SLEEVES! STICK OUT THAT CHIN!
PICK YOUR BUTT UP OFF THE GROUND
AND SAY...
OH,

LOOK FOR THE SILVER RAINBOW
IF GRAY CLOUDS RAIN ON YOUR PARADE!
BEFORE IT PASSES BY, THE SUN'LL COME OUT
AND BLUES ARE GONNA FADE!

BE A COCK-EYED OCCULIST!
WHISTLE A HAPPY SONG!

EV'RYTHING'S COMIN' UP CHRYSANTHEMUMS!
WHY DON'T YOU HUM ALONG?
YELL HALLELUJAH, COME ON GET GIDDY,
'CAUSE LIFE IS A CABERNET!
TOMORROW, TOMORROW,
THERE'S ALWAYS TOMORROW!
TOMORROW IS ANOTHER DAY!

> *(The* **CHORUS BOYS** *re-join her, selling like mad.)*

CAROL ANN.

YOU GOTTA CLIMB EV'RY LADDER!

PUT ON A HAPPY COAT!

WORK THE SUNNY SIDE OF THE AVENUE!

AND REACH THAT UNREACHABLE NOTE!

SO LET A SMILE BE YOUR BAZOOKA
TO BLAST ALL THE BLAHS AWAY!
TOMORROW, TOMORROW!

CHORUS BOYS.

CLIMB EV'RY LADDER

COAT!

CHORUS BOYS.

YEAH!

CAROL ANN.

THERE'S ALWAYS TOMORROW!

CHORUS BOYS.

YEAH!

CAROL ANN.

TOMORROW...

CHORUS BOYS.
> YEAH!!

CAROL ANN. So become a subscriber to the Melody Barn's next fabulous season! And remember–what you saw tonight is just the tip of the icebox!

> ...IS ANOTHER DAY!

> > *(The* **CHORUS BOYS** *lift a sign up and over her – bumping her head piece. The sign reads, "Help Save Musical Comedy!" On the number's button they flip the sign, delivering a final message: "SUBSCRIBE!")*

> ...PRESCRIBE!!!

> > *(Blackout.)*

[MUSIC NO. 12 "NOT ALL MAN"]

> > *(The curtain rises. A tiled half-wall extends into the wings. A large arrow on it points off the "SHOWERS." Behind the wall appears a hunky* **GUY**, *a towel around his neck, his torso bare. Toweling off, he sings fifties style.)*

GUY (TAYLOR).
> AH-OOH-AH-HA-OH,
> WHOA, WHOA, WHOA, WHOA!
> I'M ALWAYS HERE AT THE GYM.
> I-I-I CAN PUMP IRON FOR HOURS.
> BUT NO ONE WILL SPOT ME ON THE BENCH PRESS.
> AND THEY LOOK AT ME FUNNY IN THE SHOWERS.
> WHEN THE GUYS GO FOR BEER THEY LEAVE ME OU-OU-OUT.
> LATELY, IT'S SOMETHING I'M WORRIED ABOUT.

> > *(He walks around the half-wall, revealing that he's a* **CENTAUR** *half man, half horse. The joke is: he's never looked over his shoulder*

*and seen what is obvious to everyone else at
first glance.)*

CENTAUR.

    I WANT TO BE LIKED, I WANT TO BELONG;
    BUT I CAN'T FIGHT THE FEELING THAT THERE'S
      SOMETHING WRONG.
    WHY DO THEY SAY I'M NOT ALL MAN?

    I WANT TO RUN WILD AND ROLL IN THE HAY,
    BUT THERE'S A LITTLE PART OF ME THAT'S SAYING "NAY."
    WHY DO THEY SAY I'M NOT ALL MAN?

    I'M CONFUSED, BUT I'M NOT STUPID
    BACK IN SCHOOL I WAS HEAD OF THE CLA-'ASS.
    STILL, IT'S HARD TO STAY CLEARHEADED
    WHEN YOU FEEL LIKE A HORSE'S ASS!

    I GOT MUSCLES TO BURN, A STUDLY PHYSIQUE,
    YOU MUST ADMIT MY SILHOUETTE IS CLASSIC GREEK.
    WHY DO THEY SAY I'M NOT ALL MAN?

    I FEEL PULLED IN TWO DIRECTIONS,
    AND IT'S THROWN MY LIFE OFF COURSE.
    'CAUSE PART OF ME'S HUNG UP ON FITTING IN,
    AND PART OF ME'S HUNG LIKE...

...a jury with a nagging doubt... You know what I
mean? It's terrible!

    I GOT MASCULINE CHARMS TO BE RECKONED WITH
    SO WHY DO PEOPLE LOOK AT ME AND SAY, "OH, MYTH..."

I don't get it!

    WHY DO THEY SAY... WHY DO THEY SAY... WHY DO THEY
      SAY I'M NOT...

    (He goes for a big final note and coughs.)

Sorry, I'm a little hoarse.

    ALL MAN?

    (Blackout. Curtain.)

[MUSIC NO. 13 "TORCH SONG – PART 2: 'MIKE'"]

(JACOB enters with the chair, exactly as before. He sits, pulls out a bigger chiffon scarf, and begins shyly.)

JACOB.
EV'RYONE I LOVE IS ALWAYS, ALWAYS UNATTAINABLE.
WHY DO I WANT WHAT I CAN'T HAVE?
IT'S UNEXPLAINABLE.
THESE FEELINGS THAT I FEEL
DEFY ALL COMMON SENSE.
I'M OBSESSED WHAT CAN I DO?
I'M MADE FOR YOU, MIKE PENCE!

MIKE...
WHAT'S NOT TO LIKE?
I FEEL YOUR HEAT, SO LET THE FEVER SPIKE!
YOU COME FROM INDIANA, I'M AN EAST COAST LADDIE –
DOESN'T IT MAKE SENSE YOU'D BE MY "HOOSIER DADDY"?

MIKE
MAY LIGHTNING STRIKE:
I'D LOVE TO BE THE MAMIE TO YOUR IKE.
WE'LL BE SUPER CLOSE, AND I CAN HARDLY WAIT!
TRULY INTERTWINED – YOU KNOW, LIKE CHURCH AND
    STATE.

MIKE
ZOOM DOWN MY PIKE.
YOU BE THE BIKER, LET ME BE THE BIKE!
EXPAND YOUR BOUNDARIES, IT WON'T HURT YOU
GET WITH MY PROGRAM – I'LL CONVERT YOU.
I'LL GIVE YOUR TIGHTY-WHITEYS QUITE A HIKE!
BUT THAT'S PIE IN THE SKY WHEN YOU CARRY A TORCH
    FOR A GUY
LIKE MY MAN
MIKE.

(Blackout.)

[MUSIC NO. 14 "GARDEN OF EDEN"]

("Crossover #3 Adam and Steve.")

*(Music. The curtain rises to reveal the **TREE OF KNOWLEDGE**. A huge **SNAKE** sinuously coils around the trunk. The **TREE**'s upstretched branches are trimmed with paper leaves and shiny apples. Beside it, **TAYLOR** – as a fig-leaf-clad **ADAM** – holds an apple.)*

ADAM.
IN ANOTHER GARDEN JUST ACROSS FROM EDEN,
RISING FROM TWISTED ROOTS,
GREW A MIGHTY TREE THAT WAS HEAVY LADEN
WITH LOTS OF FORBIDDEN FRUITS.

THE SNAKE (FRANK'S VOICE).
OH, FORBIDDEN FRUITS...
THE SWEETEST TREAT OF ALL...

*(From offstage there is a huge, prolonged and deafening crash. The black-clad **PUPPETEER** pulls off his hood. It's **FRANK**. He drops the snake puppet, leaving it dangling from the **TREE**. **ADAM** and the **TREE** both do big physical reactions, and the **TREE** turns front to reveal it's **BRIAN**. There's a cut-out in the trunk for his face. He wears big clown-shoe "roots" on his feet. He brings his tree branch arms down in disgust. Once again he's left wearing an outfit in which it's virtually impossible to maintain any dignity. **HOWARD** dashes across from right and exits left. Sensing an imminent explosion from **BRIAN**, **FRANK** and **TAYLOR** exit.)*

BRIAN. I can't work this way! Howard!

(**BRIAN** *throws the foliage he's been holding to the floor.* **HOWARD** *re-enters. He's still in the Centaur pants – he was the back end.*)

HOWARD. Brian! What was that crash?

BRIAN. Someone dropped an earring... How the hell should I know?

(*He walks* **HOWARD** *downstage.*)

...But let's talk about something more important. Howard, I have not spent the last fifteen years in this business to play a tree that faces upstage!

HOWARD. But, Brian, you specifically said you wanted a big number with a boa...

BRIAN. (*Laughing mirthlessly, he puts his hand in the puppet snake's head, and lets it laugh for him.*) I'm hysterical. This is not what I had in mind! Howard, I have my pride.

(*He cuts off the audience before they can laugh.*)

...Don't! (*Back to* **HOWARD**.) I don't know how I let you talk me into this! But you can forget about that finale, little mister.

(**BRIAN** *starts off.*)

HOWARD. Brian, please... Wait a minute.

(**BRIAN** *uses the snake to direct a vicious hiss at* **HOWARD**, *then exits.* **HOWARD**, *at a loss, turns to the audience.*)

Well, um... Ladies and gentlemen, it looks like we won't be doing the "Adam and Steve" sketch after all. Things aren't going quite the way I planned tonight. I feel like Jeffrey Cordoba in *The Bandwagon*. When his big production number implodes? You know, with

Cyd Charisse and Fred Astaire...? Anyway, since I am the one in charge here, I guess it's up to me to figure out what I want to do...

> (*Lights zoom in to a pin spot on* **HOWARD**'s *face. Psycho nightmare piano chords.*)

MISS ROUNDHOLE'S VOICE. *(Voice over.)* "How about Garden Supply"?

> (*The lights restore.* **TAYLOR** *enters, still in his fig-leaf*)

TAYLOR. Howard, the guys need to know... Where do we go from here?

HOWARD. *(Snapping back to reality.)* Oh! Um...let's move on to the first act finale. Taylor, would you introduce the next number? I've got to go push on that set-piece!

> (**HOWARD** *exits, taking the tree branches* **BRIAN** *left behind. Gamely,* **TAYLOR** *wings it.*)

TAYLOR. And now, ladies and gentlemen, *When Pigs Fly* puts the "riot" in "Patriotism" with a Valentine to some of America's major talking heads...

[MUSIC NO. 15 "COLORADO – INTRO"]

CONSERVATIVE VOICES. *(Voice over, overlapping.)* ...And that is why Indiana is introducing the Religious Freedom and Restoration Act! No business owner should be forced to provide services that contradict his or her religious beliefs! ...Michigan House Bill 4188: No adoption agency shall be required to place a child in a same-sex household in conflict with that agency's statement of faith... North Carolina's Public Facilities Privacy and Security Act will mandate that... And that is why I urge you to support Oregon's Measure 9, the Abnormal Behavior Initiative... Act now before this insidious threat to Traditional American Family Values... These people have an agenda! Colorado's

Amendment 2 states there shall be no "special rights" for any class of citizen! ...

[MUSIC NO. 16 "COLOR OUT OF COLORADO"]

(During this, a **BAND LEADER** *– resplendent in a uniform trimmed with gold epaulets and shiny braid – strolls on and listens, bemused. Then he blows a whistle, cutting off the babble. He's an upbeat and appealing Music Man with a twinkle in his eye and a reassuring chuckle.)*

BAND LEADER (FRANK).
IN STATE AFTER STATE THE LEGISLATURE
WANTS TO REGULATE HUMAN NATURE.
THERE'S FOLKS FROM SEA TO SHINING SEA
WHO'D LIKE TO TELL YOU WHO TO BE.
THEY CAN PASS ALL THE STATUTES THAT THEY PLEASE –
ACORNS WON'T GROW INTO MAPLE TREES.
BESIDES, THOSE DIFFERENCES THEY HATE
ARE THE STRENGTH THAT MAKES THIS COUNTRY GREAT.
ONLY FOOLS WOULD WRITE THOSE LAWS.
THEY SIMPLY CAN'T SUCCEED BECAUSE...

YOU CAN'T TAKE THE "COLOR" OUT OF COLORADO.
YOU CAN'T TAKE THE "MARY" OUT OF MARY-LAND.
AS JOHN PHILIP SOUSA SAID, "I CAN'T MARCH
IF I CAN'T HEAR THE BOYS IN THE BAND!"

YOU CAN'T TAKE THE "SISSY" OUT OF MISSISSIPPI.
HE'S THERE AND HE'S GOING TO STAY.
AND SO Q.E.D.
IT'S AS PLAIN AS ABC:
YOU NEED "US" TO MAKE THE U.S.A.

(During the next chorus, three more **BAND MEMBERS** *enter one at a time and join in.)*

TAYLOR.

> YOU CAN'T KICK OUR ASSES OUT OF MASSACHUSETTS OR
> SUBTRACT THE TEN PERCENT FROM TENNESSEE.

TAYLOR & FRANK.

> UTAH COULD NEVER BE THE BEEHIVE STATE IF THE
> HAIRDRESSERS WENT ABSENTEE.

HOWARD.

> YOU CAN'T RUN THE HOMOS OUT OF OKLAHOMA. (YEOW!)
> IT'S THEIR HOME AND THEY WON'T GO AWAY.

TAYLOR, FRANK & HOWARD.

> IN THE LAND OF THE FREE DIVERSITY'S THE KEY.
> YOU NEED "US" TO MAKE THE U.S.A.

JACOB.

> SHH!

ALL.

> WHO WILL NEVER BE PASSE IN OLD EL PASO?
> WHO WILL ALWAYS KNOW WHAT'S NEW IN NEW
> ORLEANS?

JACOB.

> CHICAGO WITH NO "CHIC" WOULD BE BORING IN A WEEK.
> AND YOU CAN'T HAVE NEW YORK CITY WITHOUT QUEENS!

ALL.

> RIGHT!
> YOU CANNOT REPLACE THOSE STATEN ISLAND FERRIES.
> AND WHO'LL ALWAYS KEEP SANTA FE?
> YES, WE'RE PROUD TO STATE
> WE HELP MAKE THIS COUNTRY GREAT!
> YOU NEED "US" TO MAKE THE U.S.A.

> *(They march off as the black curtains part
> to reveal* **BRIAN** *as* **LADY LIBERTY.** *She comes
> down stage to sing an ad-lib verse.)*

LADY LIBERTY.

> GO ON, TAKE THE "VIRGIN" OUT OF WEST VIRGINIA.

TAKE THE "ORGI" OUT OF GEORGIA, IF YOU MUST.
YOU CAN DRIVE THE EVIL OUT OF WISCON-"SIN"
AND LEAVE ILLINOIS' "ILLS" IN THE DUST
YOU COULD TRY TO TAKE THE "K-Y" FROM KENTUCKY,
THOUGH I DOUBT THAT YOU'LL GET VERY FAR!

(The **BAND LEADER** *returns. They harmonize.)*

BAND LEADER & LADY LIBERTY.
BUT YOU'LL NEVER TAKE THE COLOR OUT OF
COLORADO –

BAND LEADER.
DON'T YOU REALIZE WHO WE ARE...?

*(***LADY LIBERTY** *exits.)*

WE'RE THE FRIENDLY TELLER AT THE BANK.
WE'RE THE TEACHER AT YOUR SUNDAY SCHOOL.
WE'RE THE GUY WHO FIXED YOUR WATER TANK.
WE'RE THE CUTE NEW LIFEGUARD AT THE POOL.
WE'RE THE NICE YOUNG MAN WHO BOUGHT YOUR CAR.
WE'RE THE LADY SINGING ON THE RADIO.
WE'RE YOUR FAV'RITE DAYTIME TV STAR.

(Now the **OTHERS** *return, dressed for various
occupations – a doctor, a construction worker,
an athlete, and a businessman.)*

ALL KINDS OF PEOPLE YOU ALREADY KNOW.

BAND LEADER & ALL.
WE'RE DOCTORS, LAWYERS,
MOVERS, SHAKERS,
FRIENDS AND NEIGHBORS,
POLICY MAKERS.
AND REMEMBER THIS ABOUT US:

*(The upstage black rises to reveal a huge
American flag.)*

AMERICA COULDN'T DO WITHOUT US.

THINK OF PROVINCETOWN, KEY WEST, AND SAN FRANCISCO.

WITHOUT US THEY'D BE A LOT MORE LIKE FORT WAYNE.

WE'RE PART OF AMERICA THE BEAUTIFUL.

REMEMBER HER FRUITED PLAIN!

WHEN YOU'RE MARCHING TO A MASTER ORCHESTRATION,

YOU MUST LET ALL THE INSTRUMENTS PLAY!

JUST TO LEAVE NO DOUBT,

ONE MORE TIME WE'LL SPELL IT OUT:

YOU NEED "US" TO MAKE THE U.S.A.!

YOU NEED "US" TO MAKE THE U.S.A.!

(Confetti canons shoot red, white, and blue streamers on the button.)

[MUSIC NO. 17 "COLORADO BOWS"]

(Blackout. Curtain.)

End of Act I

ACT II

[MUSIC NO. 18 "VANITY – INTRO"]

[MUSIC NO. 19 "WEAR YOUR VANITY WITH PRIDE"]

(The curtain rises on an outrageously costumed and wigged RESTORATION ERA DANDY. *He stands between two vanity tables, which are trimmed with flounces and support large open "mirrors." As he poses and preens, he is joined by a* SECOND DANDY, *and then a* THIRD. *They strut for the audience, trying to outdo each other. They are ridiculous overdressed fops.)*

DANDY #1 (HOWARD).

IF YOU WANT TO CATCH THE EYE, YOU'VE GOT TO PAY THE PRICE.

LACED AND CINCHED,

PATCHED AND PINCHED –

IT'S A NASTY BUS'NESS LOOKING NICE.

DANDY #2 (FRANK).

I KNOW MY COLLAR'S TIGHT ENOUGH WHEN I BEGIN TO BLACK OUT.

DANDY #3 (TAYLOR).

AND HEELS THAT GIVE ME HEIGHT ENOUGH

ARE SURE TO THROW MY BACK OUT.

ALL THREE.

YET WHEN WE ENTER, ALL HEADS TURN,

OUR VICTORY IS PLAIN!

THESE ARE THE WAGES THAT WE EARN
THROUGH SUFFERING AND PAIN.

> *(Various jabs of pain briefly crumple* **ALL**
> **THREE.** *Clearly they are looking fabulous at
> the cost of great personal discomfort. They
> pull themselves up bravely and continue.)*

(OW!) WE WEAR OUR VANITY WITH PRIDE,
HIDING OUR DISCOMFORT WELL.

DANDY #3.

THERE'S A SWEET REWARD;
WE'RE ENVIED AND ADORED,

DANDY #2.

BUT TO LOOK THIS HEAVENLY
WE'VE GOT TO GO THROUGH HELL.

ALL.

OH! WE WEAR OUR VANITY WITH PRIDE,
THAT'S THE BIRTHRIGHT OF OUR SEX.

DANDY #1.

EACH CAN EXERCISE HIS OPTION AS A MALE
TO EMULATE THE LION'S MANE AND APE THE PEACOCK'S
TAIL.

ALL.

WE LET MOTHER NATURE BE OUR GUIDE!
WE WEAR OUR VANITY WITH PRIDE.

> **(DANDIES** #2 *and* #3 *pull back the upstage
> traveller, revealing two* **LADIES** [**BRIAN**
> *and* **JACOB**], *who are wearing elaborately
> trimmed period bodices, but no skirts, their
> legs exposed, showgirl style. On their heads
> they wear frilly mob-caps. The* **LADIES**
> *quickly take their places at the dressing
> tables and begin primping.)*

DANDY #1.

> FASHION MAKES DEMANDS ON THEM THAT NO ONE
> COMPREHENDS.
> SQUEEZE AND TUCK,
> POKE AND PLUCK –
> THE ROUTINE NEVER ENDS.

DANDIES #2 & #3.

> WHAT'S THEIR BEAUTY SECRET?

LADY #1 (BRIAN).

> A MASK OF PUREED PEACHES!

LADY #2 (JACOB).

> A DAILY DOSE OF ARSENIC!

DANDY #1.

> AND THEN – BI-WEEKLY – LEECHES!

TWO LADIES.

> EEWW! AND THOUGH TO TOUCH THOSE SLIMY THINGS
> WE'D LIKE TO WEAR A GLOVE,
> EACH VISIT TO OUR MIRROR BRINGS
> ANOTHER CHANCE TO FALL IN LOVE...

>> (**DANDIES** #2 *and* #3 *go behind the* **LADIES** *and mime lacing up their corsets.*)

> WE WEAR OUR VANITY WITH PRIDE.
> STIFLING THE CONSTANT ACHE.

LADY #2.

> THOUGH WE'RE STABBED BY STAYS
> TILL OUR EYES BEGIN TO GLAZE,

>> (*The* **LADIES** *react as* **DANDIES** #1 *and* #2 *pull their corsets tighter and tighter. The final yank causes them to shriek.*)

> THESE ARE LITTLE SACRIFICES EV'RY GIRL MUST MAKE.

(**DANDY** #1 *gives a brisk double clap and
sends* **DANDIES** #2 *and* #3 *off-stage.*)

TWO LADIES.

WE WEAR OUR VANITY WITH PRIDE,
WE GRIT OUR TEETH, AND DON'T ASK WHY.

LADY #1.

THINK OF CHINESE LADIES BINDING UP THEIR FEET
AND LIP PLATES ON THE AFRICAN ELITE.
IT'S THEIR DUTY TO BE BEAUTIFIED!

TWO LADIES.

SO THEY WEAR THEIR VANITY WITH PRIDE.

(**DANDIES** #2 *and* #3 *return with huge
powdered wigs. The* **LADIES** *remove their
mob-caps and the wigs are lowered into place.
They are pleased with the effect.* **DANDIES** #2
and #3 *remove the mirrors from the vanity
tables, tilting them so the* **LADIES** *can get a
better view of themselves. They then pass
the mirrors into the wings. Through all this*
DANDY #1 *pumps out clouds of perfume from
a gold sprayer. As everyone chokes, he fixes a
cool eye on the audience.*)

DANDY #1.

BUT! AS SLAVES TO VANITY, WE CAN' T COMPETE WITH
    YOU!

DANDY #2.

PUMPED AND PUFFED,
RIPPED AND BUFFED –
IT'S GRUESOME WHAT YOU DO.

DANDY #3.

STRAPPED INTO YOUR TORTURE RACKS
YOU GRUNT OUT TWENTY "REPS."

LADY #1.

> THEN, INVITING HEART ATTACKS,
> YOU JUMP ABOUT ON STEPS!

LADY #2.

> BURNING FLESH UNTIL IT'S TAN,
> TO US THAT'S RATHER ODD.

DANDY #1.

> YOU'VE STUMBLED ON A BEAUTY PLAN
> DESIGNED BY THE MARQUIS DE SADE!
> BUT...

> > *(Musical interlude.* **DANDY** #1 *exits. The* **LADIES** *stand and lift the vanity tables. Assisted by* **DANDIES,** #1 *and* #2, *they hang the tables from hooks at their hips. They are now literally "wearing" their vanity tables. The* **DANDIES** *pull out cords that have been passed through rings along the tops of the vanity table flounces. The flounces fall into full elaborately trimmed skirts that match the* **LADIES'** *bodices. The* **DANDIES** *and* **LADIES** *parade grandly.)*

QUARTET.

> YOU WEAR YOUR VANITY WITH PRIDE,
> VYING FOR THE LIMELIGHT'S GLARE.
> WITH EACH STOMACH CRUNCH
> AND PROTEIN POWDER LUNCH
> YOU PROVE YOU'RE IN THE POWER OF THE MANIA WE
> > SHARE:
> YOU WEAR YOUR VANITY WITH PRIDE,
> SINGLE-MINDED IN YOUR QUEST.
> TO BE BLESSED BY BEAUTY, FIRST YOU MUST BE CURSED.
> TO LOOK YOUR BEST, YOU HAVE TO BRAVE THE WORST!
> YOU CAN TAKE EACH LITTLE ACHE IN STRIDE
> WHEN YOU WEAR YOUR VANITY,

YOUR INSANITY,
YOUR SUPERIORITY TO MERE HUMANITY,
WEAR YOUR VANITY
WITH PRIDE!
OOH! AAH!

*(A final twinge of pain crumples them all
for a moment. Then they pull themselves up
one more time, waving regally as the curtain
falls.)*

[MUSIC NO. 20 "VANITY TAG"]

[MUSIC NO. 21 "LAST ONE PICKED"]

*(**HOWARD**, dressed for a high school reunion –
tie and blazer with a "Hi, My Name is
Howard" sticker on the lapel – leans across
the upright piano, which conceals his lower
half. A "Welcome Alumni" banner has been
released in the scaffolding above him.)*

HOWARD.
CLINK A GLASS AND WIPE YOUR EYE
FOR MY BYGONE DAYS AT SPRINGBROOK HIGH
AND THE CLASS I LEARNED TO DREAD –
THAT EGO-BUSTER THEY CALLED PHYS ED.
BASKETBALL, BASEBALL, FOOTBALL, STICKBALL,
VOLLEYBALL, DODGEBALL, TETHERBALL, KICKBALL;
PLAYING WAS HELL, BUT WORST OF ALL.
WAS THE RITUAL THAT CAME FIRST OF ALL.

*(There's a jarring school bell and a light
strobes as his coat and tie break away. He's
propelled to center in a baggy gym uniform.)*

COACH. *(Voice over.)* All right, captains! Choose your
teams!

HOWARD.
LAST ONE PICKED.

NON-ATHLETIC.
LAST ONE PICKED.
AT SPORTS I WAS PATHETIC.
OTHER KIDS COULD TUMBLE AND RUN,
BUT MY COORDINATION WAS TOTALLY "UN."

SIX GUYS LEFT.
STOMACH SINKING.
THREE GUYS LEFT.
MY SELF-ESTEEM WAS SHRINKING!
FELT SO ASHAMED I COULD HAVE CRIED –
NOBODY WANTED ME ON THEIR SIDE.

HOW MANY NOTES DID I FORGE TO SAY,
"PLEASE EXCUSE HOWARD FROM GYM TODAY.
HE WRENCHED HIS BACK, HIS COLON'S SPASTIC,
HE'S HYPOGLYCEMIC, AND HIS KNEECAPS ARE PLASTIC."

I WAS THE LAST ONE PICKED.
REJECTED BY THE RABBLE.
LAST ONE PICKED.
(I COULD BEAT 'EM ALL AT SCRABBLE!)
MY BRAINS DIDN'T DO ME A BIT OF GOOD:
THE BOTTOM OF THE BARREL WAS WHERE I STOOD.

BUT TIME WENT BY, AND I MET YOU
AND LEARNED A TEAM COULD CONSIST OF TWO.
THE WAY I WAS WAS A-OK!
AND WHO CARED ABOUT KIDS' GAMES ANYWAY?

LAST ONE PICKED!
THE PAST IS PAST NOW.
LAST ONE PICKED!
AT LAST I'M NOT THE LAST NOW!
I'M FIRST DRAFT CHOICE ON A WINNING TEAM
LIKE I ALWAYS DREAMED I'D BE.
IMAGINE MY SURPRISE
WHEN – OUT OF ALL THOSE OTHER GUYS –
YOU
PICKED
ME!

(Blackout.)

[MUSIC NO. 22 "THE NERD"]

(Curtain rises to reveal **JACOB** *as a* **NERDY COMICON FANBOY** *– glasses, loads of passes on lanyards around his neck, top shirt-button buttoned. He is enthusiastic and likable. He recites.)*

THE NERD.
   I'M A FANBOY SUPER GEEK
   COMIC CON WAS JUST LAST WEEK!
   ALL THOSE HEROES ON DISPLAY:
   SOME OF THEM, LIKE ME, ARE GAY.
   MUTANTS AND FANTASTIC CREATURES
   EACH POSSESSING MAGIC FEATURES!
   I'M PROUD TO SAY, SOME SUPERPOWERS
   SEEM TO BE UNIQUELY OURS!

   (During the course of the number, the **NERD** *will be visited by three fantastic gay* **SUPERHEROES** *who school him in how to access the gay superpowers within him. All three costumes feature over-the-head masks in bold, distinctive shapes with large cut-outs around the eyes. The masks end at the upper lip, so the actors' jaws are unimpeded. The first* **SUPERHERO** *enters.)*

[MUSIC NO. 23 "FREAK"]

THE MONSTER (FRANK).
   I'M YOUR PARTY MONSTER
   DANCIN'S WHAT I GOT TO DO!
   WHEN YOU BUST LOOSE
   WHO TURNS THE JUICE UP?
   ME!
   I'M A PART OF YOU!

SCENE MAKER!
TREND SETTER!
ALL-ROUND ATTENTION GETTER!

(One-two-three)

(Rap.)

YOU GOT MAGIC FEET!
GO ON! SHAKE THAT SEAT!
BEAT THE COMPETITION ALL HOLLOW!
WE GOT ALL WE NEED!
MOVES AND SPEED!
WE LEAD!
LET THE OTHERS FOLLOW!
5-6-7-8

DOMINATE THE DANCE FLOOR!
THROW DOWN YOUR TECHNIQUE!
GO ON, HAVE A BALL!
CALL UPON YOUR INNER-FREAK!

(THE MONSTER *exits as the second* **SUPERHERO** *takes center stage.)*

THE DIVA (BRIAN).

I'M THE SECRET DIVA
HIDDEN IN YOUR INNER SOUL.
IF YOU'VE BEEN HARMED
DON'T BE ALARMED
STAND BACK –
I TAKE CONTROL!
DEMANDING!
DRAMATIC!
TRASH TALK
THAT'S OPERATIC!

(Rap.)

I'LL FULMINATE

AND GESTICULATE,
I'LL CREATE ONE HELLUVA SCENE!
BY THE TIME WE'RE DONE,
THEY'LL BE ON THE RUN.
IT'S FUN!
I'M YOUR DRAMA QUEEN!

IF YOU WANT RESPECT, DEAR!
DON'T BE MILD AND MEEK!
GET UP OFF YOUR BUM,
SUMMON UP YOUR INNER FREAK!

    *(***THE MONSTER*** returns.)*

THE NERD, THE MONSTER, & THE DIVA.
THERE ARE SUPER POWERS!
IN GAY DNA!
CRACK THAT ACCESS CODE,
WE'LL TAKE YOU A LONG, LONG, LONG, LONG, LONG, WAY!
    AY AY AY!

> *(They move upstage where the upstage black
> rises just enough to let* **THE BEAST** *emerge
> from between* **HOWARD***'s legs.* **THE MONSTER**
> *and* **THE DIVA** *remain onstage for the rest of
> the number.)*

THE BEAST (HOWARD).
I'M THE ALTER EGO
THAT YOU HAVEN'T QUITE RELEASED.
BUT WHEN YOU DREAM,
YOU WANT TO BE ME.
YES!

I'M ONE SEXY BEAST!	**BRIAN & FRANK.**
ASSERTIVE.	OOH
BUT GENTLE.	
WILDLY EXPERIMENTAL!	

(One-two-three)

(Rap.)

LET THE GAMES COMMENCE
FEEL MY CONFIDENCE
WATCH A LINE OF LOVERS APPROACH YOU.
LOSE YOUR FEAR.
LET IT DISAPPEAR!
I'M HERE!
JUST LET ME COACH YOU!
OWN YOUR WHOLE PERSONA:
FAN-BOY SCI-FI GEEK!
YOU'LL BE HUNKIFIED,
GUIDED BY YOUR INNER FREAK.

ALL.
(FREAK FREAK FREAK)

THE NERD.
AHHH!

THE MONSTER, THE DIVA & THE BEAST.
YASSS!
WHY BE UNSURE AND NERVOUS?
WE'RE HERE AT YOUR SERVICE!

THE MONSTER.
BOOGIE TILL THE DAWN,
WE MONSTERS PARTY ON!

THE DIVA.
DON'T BE PUSHED ABOUT,
LET YOUR DIVA OUT!

THE BEAST.
YOU'RE HOT TO SAY THE LEAST
BEAUTIES LOVE A BEAST!

THE MONSTER, THE DIVA & THE BEAST.
TRUST YOUR QUEER MYSTIQUE,
JUST EMBRACE YOUR INNER FREAK!
FREAK!

[MUSIC NO. 23A "FREAK PLAYOFF"]

(Blackout. Curtain.)

(HOWARD has ducked under the curtain before it falls. He takes off his Beast mask and holds it as he addresses the audience.)

HOWARD. The truth is, ladies and gentlemen, fabulous creatures have always walked among us. But it wasn't that long ago – some of you may even remember it – when all that fabulosity had to be kept under wraps.

[MUSIC NO. 24 "SAM AND ME"]

(HOWARD exits as the curtain rises to reveal a vaguely retro TAYLOR – thin lapels, skinny tie, Vitalised hair. There's a whiff of Madison Avenue about him. He appears to be the highly-strung and excitable type. He is, in fact, DARREN from Bewitched – but the audience won't figure this out until the end of the song.)

DARREN.
I LIVE OUT IN SUBURBIA:
COOKIE-CUTTER HOUSES, COOKIE-CUTTER LIVES GOING ON INSIDE...
MY SPLIT LEVEL'S LIKE ALL THE REST:
GRASS MOWED, TWO-CAR GARAGE, FLAGSTONE WALK, FRESH PAINT...
BUT I CAN GUARANTEE YOU, IF THE NEIGHBORS KNEW THE TRUTH –
HALF OF THEM WOULD CUT ME DEAD,
THE OTHER HALF WOULD FAINT!
WHO WOULD THINK TO LOOK AT ME,
CONSERVATIVE AS I AM,
THAT IN MY LITTLE TRACT HOUSE,
HAPPINESS IS JUST A THING CALLED... SAM?

After all, it's 1967. Attitudes are changing – but not that fast!

SECRETS AREN'T EASY-KEEPING THEM STRESSFUL.
STILL, THE THRILL HAS HELPED TO MAKE OUR
    PARTNERSHIP SUCCESSFUL.
WE'VE CHOSEN A LIFE-STYLE HUSBAND AND WIFE
    STYLE...
WELL, IT WORKS FOR SAM AND ME!

IT'S LIFE ON A TIGHTROPE, EXPOSURE SEEMS TO HOVER.
FEELS LIKE NEARLY EV'RY WEEK WE ALMOST BLOW OUR
    COVER.
BUT SOMEHOW THE TENSION GIVES LOVE A NEW
    DIMENSION...
WELL, IT WORKS FOR SAM AND ME.

I GO TO WORK, SAM CLEANS AND COOKS.
THAT'S OUR DEAL, AND IT WORKS OUT GREAT.
I'M A STICKLER FOR HOW THINGS "LOOK,"
SO WHEN THE BOSS COMES TO DINNER, SAM PLAYS IT
    "STRAIGHT."

SAM'S PALS POP IN OFTEN; THEY'RE GAUDY AND THEY'RE
    RECKLESS.
IF PEARLS ARE CAUSED BY IRRITATION, I SHOULD BE A
    NECKLACE!
DON'T KNOW WHY ON EARTH IT
SHOULD FEEL LIKE IT'S WORTH IT...
BUT IT WORKS FOR SAM AND ME.

I say, "Sam, please – the kaftans...the bitchery! Can't they tone it down a little?" "Hey, they're *family*," Sam says. Hmph! Some family! Talk about your crazy aunties and funny uncles!

THE MAILMAN SNOOPS, THE NEIGHBORS PEEK,
BUT WE KEEP THE CURTAINS DRAWN!
MY MOM AND DAD WOULD REALLY FREAK
IF THEY EVER FIGURED OUT WHAT'S GOING ON.

HEY, DON'T RUSH TO JUDGMENT! DON'T CALL OUR
    CHOICES TRAGIC!

WE MAY BE IN THE CLOSET, BUT THE CHEMISTRY IS
    MAGIC!
FOR US, IT'S THE RIGHT LIFE,
A WILD NICK-AT-NIGHT-LIFE.
THAT'S THE KICKER, YOU SEE.
IN SPITE OF ALL THE FITS I'VE PITCHED,
THE COURSE OF TRUE LOVE CAN'T BE SWITCHED.
THOUGH I'M BOTHERED, BEWILDERED, BEDEVILED TO A
    DEGREE...
I'M STILL BEWITCHED!
AND IT WORKS FOR SAMANTHA AND ME!

> *(Just before the musical button,* **ENDORA**
> *appears in a cloud of smoke.)*

ENDORA (BRIAN). Oh, shut up, Durwood!

> *(She zaps him and he dashes off.)*

Mortals! And he's not even the original one!

> *(With her trademark swoop of the arms she
> zaps herself away.)*

> *(Blackout. Curtain.)*

[MUSIC NO. 25 "BABY JANE CROSSOVER"]

> *(A vaudeville vamp.* **JACOB** *enters as* **BETTE
> DAVIS** *in full* **BABY JANE** *regalia. He curtsies
> and looks expectantly towards the pass-door.
> When no one appears, he rolls his eyes, goes
> off, and returns – cradling a life-sized* **JOAN
> CRAWFORD** *rag doll.* **JOAN** *tips her head to
> the audience, then whispers to* **JACOB**.*)

BABY JANE. What? You're ready to do our number?

> *(***JOAN** *nods.)*

Mister conductor, if you please!

*(The **PIANIST** plays an arpeggio and turns his page.)*

BOX OFFICE POISON LOOKING FOR WORK
WHO'S IN A "STRAIGHTJACKET" ACTING BERSERK?

(The musical accompaniment has stopped.)

PIANIST. Psst... Jacob...

*(The **PIANIST** motions **JACOB** over. There's a big post-it stuck to a page in the score. The **PIANIST** hands the note over to **JACOB**, who reads it, unceremoniously dumps **JOAN** in a heap, and lets out a blood curdling.)*

JACOB. HOWARD!!!

*(**HOWARD** appears, dressed in work coveralls, wearing a wardrobe mistress' apron, pockets filled with pincushions, thread, tape measures, etc. The strain of the evening's problems is starting to show.)*

HOWARD. What is it, Jay?

JACOB. Howard, does the name Ed Goldschneider mean anything to you?

HOWARD. It sort of rings a bell...

JACOB. Ed Goldschneider. The man who laboriously wrote out the full forty-piece orchestra score for this show? Of which we are only using the piano and drum parts, because you forgot that musicians don't work for free? Well, Ed Goldschneider hasn't been paid!

HOWARD. I've been having a cash flow problem.

JACOB. *(Thrusting the note at **HOWARD**.)* He's pulling a song a day until he gets a check!

HOWARD. *(Reading from the note.)* "P.S. I'm giving you a break by starting with one of Jacob's numbers..."

JACOB. Hey! *(He snatches the note back.)* Oh great! Now I've got a costume and no song. What do you want to do, Howard?

> *(Lights zoom in to a pin spot on* **HOWARD***'s face. Psycho nightmare piano chords.)*

MISS ROUNDHOLE. *(Voice over.)* Have you thought about plumbing?!!

> *(Lights restore.* **HOWARD** *hasn't snapped back.)*

JACOB. Hello! Earth to Howard! Howard, are you so broke you can't even afford to pay attention?

HOWARD. Sorry, Jacob.

JACOB. Look, Howard. Can I tell you something as a friend? Learn to think small.

HOWARD. Well, Jacob, that's really not my style...

JACOB. Small, Howard. Little. Teeny-weenie.

HOWARD. Okay, Jacob. I'll try.

> *(***JACOB*** scoops up the* **JOAN CRAWFORD** *doll, and resumes the* **BETTE DAVIS** *character.)*

JACOB. Thank you. Come on, Joan. I'll buy you a Pepsi.

> *(As they exit through the pass door* **JACOB** *accidentally on purpose slams* **JOAN** *into the doorframe. He re-positions her.)*

So sorry!

> *(***JACOB*** whacks* **JOAN** *against the doorframe again and exits with wicked laugh.* **HOWARD** *gets an idea.)*

HOWARD. Something small... I'll try. *(To the* **PIANIST***.)* Can you play me something small? I'll cue you...

[MUSIC NO. 26 "BIGGER IS BETTER"]

(The **PIANIST** *plays a high, tinkly vamp.* **HOWARD** *reaches behind the proscenium and brings on a tiny showgirl puppet. He manipulates the puppet in bumps and grinds across the stage. But somehow it's just not working for him.* **HOWARD** *signals into the wings. The curtain rises to reveal a full sized* **SHOWGIRL** *dressed identically to the puppet. Playfully, she bumps the pint-sized version – and a delighted* **HOWARD** *– into the wings.)*

SHOWGIRL (FRANK).
> BIGGER IS BETTER,
> THAT'S THE WAY TO WIDEN YOUR APPEAL.
> WHAT'S MORE DELICIOUS –
> A CEL'RY STALK? OR A TEN COURSE *(BOOM-BOOM)*
>   GOURMET MEAL?
>
> BIGGER IS BETTER,
> THAT'S A RULE TO MAKE A GIRL FEEL GREAT.
> WHAT'S MORE INVITING –
> A ONE ROOM FLAT OR A *(BOOM-BOOM, BOOM-BOOM)*
>   GRAND ESTATE?
>
> PUT ON A FEW, IT'S NOT SO BAD.
> YOUR MAN WILL LEARN TO LOVE IT.
> I'VE GOT ALL I EVER HAD –
> IN FACT, I'VE GOT A LOT MORE OF IT!
>
> BIGGER IS BETTER,
> AN AMPLE SHAPE KEEPS INT'REST EVERGREEN!
> WOULD YOU RATHER RIDE
> A POGO STICK OR A FULL *(BOOM)* STRETCH *(BOOM)*
>   LIMOUSINE?

I may have some mileage on me, but I know how to handle the curves! And talk about your dual air bags...!

> BIGGER IS BETTER,

THAT'S THE KEY TO KEEPING OUT OF HOCK.
WHAT SPARKLES MORE,
A DIAMOND CHIP? OR A FIFTEEN *(BOOM-BOOM)* CARAT
    ROCK?
BIGGER IS BETTER,
LARGE AND LUCIOUS ALWAYS GETS MY VOTE.
WHAT KEEPS YOU WARM,
A MUSKRAT MUFF? OR A *(CH-CH-CH-CH-)* CHINCHILLA
    COAT?
WHEN YOUR FIGURE STARTS TO SPREAD,
THAT'S NO CAUSE TO HATE IT.
DO WHAT ZIEGFELD DID INSTEAD –
(BOOM-BOOM, BOOM-BOOM) DECORATE IT!... CELEBRATE
    IT!

(To the **PIANIST.***)* Come on honey, I need a bigger finish!

BIGGER, *(BOOM)* IS BETTER *(BOOM)*,
TAKE THAT TIP AND LIFE KEEPS GETTING FINER!
WHAT FLOATS YOUR BOAT
A DINGHY OR A FULL *(BOOM)* RIGGED *(BOOM)* LUXURY
    LINER?
TOO MUCH OF A GOOD THING IS NEVER ENOUGH *(BOOM)*!
COME ON, BABY, STRUT YOUR STUFF!
AND THAT IS WHAT I CAME OUT HERE TO SAY.

Even my message is heavy!

BIGGER IS BETTER,
SO BETTER GET BIGGER TODAY!

And remember girls: Life is like a paycheck. A generous
figure is always nice!

YEAH!

    (Blackout. Curtain.)

    **[MUSIC NO. 27 "TORCH SONG – PART 3:
    'VLAD'"]**

*(**JACOB** enters. Same chair, an even bigger scarf.)*

JACOB.

ONCE MORE MY TWISTED, TORTURED HEART
COULD NOT BE MORE SINCERE.
NOW FOR YOU IT'S CONVALUTIN'
MR. PUTIN, DEAR...
VLAD...
I'M MORE THAN GLAD
TO HELP YOU MAYBE LIGHTEN UP A TAD.
MY LITTLE MOSCOW MULE, OUR LOVE WILL CATCH ON
    FIRE,
ONCE I PLY YOU WITH A LITTLE STOLICHNAYA...
VLAD
I GOT IT BAD.
I'D FOLLOW YOU FROM OMSK TO VOLGOGRAD.
OUR SENATE SAYS YOU HACKED US – WHAT COULD BE
    ABSURDER?
YOU DON'T HAVE THE TIME – I MEAN, YOUR SCHEDULE'S
    MURDER!
VLAD
LET'S JUST GO MAD!
THE RULES OF LOVE ARE NOT SO IRON-CLAD!
SO, PAW ME, MUSS ME UP! DEGRADE ME!
I'LL BE CRIMEA, COME INVADE ME!
LET'S SHOOT YOUR MISSILE FROM MY LAUNCHING PAD!
BUT THAT'S PIE IN THE SKY, WHEN YOU CARRY A TORCH
    FOR A GUY
LIKE MY MAN...

(Suddenly self-conscious, he stops the music.)

Oh, oh... Wait...sorry. I know what you must be thinking: "This is all so inappropriate!" I mean, what are we gonna do next? Give Mitch McConnell a big French kiss? *(He shudders.)* "Have we no pride?!" you say. "Don't we know what's going on in the world? Is all this frivolity really called for?!" Well, seriously, folks...

[MUSIC NO. 28 "LAUGHING MATTERS"]

LIVE AT FIVE AND
CNN KEEP US ALL ABREAST
OF BREAKING STORIES THAT CAN
TEND TO MAKE US ANXIOUS AND DEPRESSED.
PROBLEMS WITH NO ANSWERS
HANG ON LIKE SOME NAGGING COUGH.
AND EV'RY DAY SOME BRAND NEW "ISSUE"
REARS ITS HEAD TO PISS YOU OFF:

BAD GUYS WIN.
OPTIMISM'S WEARING THIN.
THINGS ARE SPINNING
OUT OF CONTROL.
CYNICISM'S ALL THE FAD –
WORLD EVENTS COULD MAKE US MAD AS HATTERS.
ALMOST EV'RY DAY
SOME UNDERPINNING SLIPS AWAY.
THESE AREN'T LAUGHING MATTERS.

TIME-BOMBS TICK.
PEOPLE KEEP ON GETTING SICK.
AND A NICKEL'S
NOT WORTH A CENT.
WICKEDNESS AND GREED ABOUND.
JUST AS PEACE IS GAINING GROUND
IT SHATTERS.
HATE IS HERE TO STAY.
AND JUSTICE GOES TO THOSE WHO PAY.
THESE AREN'T LAUGHING MATTERS.

THE TRUTH IS SCARIER BY FAR
THAN ANYTHING
THAT STEPHEN KING
COULD WRITE.

THE STORIES IN THE PAPER ARE
A DAILY SMALL
DECLINE AND FALL
SPELLED OUT IN BLACK AND WHITE.
WHAT TO DO?
HOW TO TAKE A BRIGHTER VIEW
WHEN YOUR NOODLE'S
TOTALLY FRIED?
HUMAN SPIRITS NEED TO BE
LEAVENED BY SOME LEVITY –
SO TAKE THOSE BLUES AND BOUNCE THEM OFF THE
    WALL.
KEEP YOUR HUMOR, PLEASE.
'CAUSE DON'T YOU KNOW, IT'S TIMES LIKE THESE
THAT LAUGHING MATTERS MOST OF ALL.

    (Lights fade.)

[MUSIC NO. 28A "WHEN PIGS DON'T FLY"]

    (Big musical intro. The curtain rises to reveal
    BRIAN *standing center in a pig costume –*
    pink velour, snout, ears, and curly tail. Over
    the costume he wears a harness attached to
    a thick rope that extends into the flies. His
    arms are folded across his chest.)

VOICE OVER. Mission control, we are ready for lift off.
Five... Four... Three... Two... One...

    (From offstage the rest of the cast tries to hoist
    him. He doesn't budge.)

HOWARD. *(Sticking his head out from the wings.)* Brian,
come on! *(Entering.)* Brian, please! It's the moment
everyone's been waiting for!

BRIAN. You want to see a pig fly? Buy me a ham sandwich
and put me on a plane to Hawaii! I *told* you this

wouldn't work. Now I'll give you till the count of three to get me out of this contraption!

(**HOWARD** *fumbles with the harness.*)

BRIAN. One!

OTHERS. *(Offstage.)* One!

BRIAN. Two!

OTHERS. *(Offstage.)* Two!

BRIAN. Three!

OTHERS. *(Offstage.)* Three!

> (*The unfastened harness is yanked up into the flies. There's a huge crash from offstage.*)

HOWARD. Sorry, guys!

BRIAN. Well, Howard, I hope you're satisfied. You wouldn't listen to me, and now here you are in front of all these people looking stupid.

HOWARD. Brian, we had to fly a pig. It's the title of the show!

> (*The **OTHERS** enter still holding the hoist rope. They nurse various scrapes and bruises.*)

BRIAN. Howard, what is this obsession with making a pig fly? The whole point is: it's *impossible*. I mean, look at your cast. Their nerves are shot. They're at the end of their rope.

> (**JACOB** *holds out the frayed rope end, demonstrating that this is literally true.*)

HOWARD. Hey, guys – I know things have gone a little off track, but come on! We'll find another way to fly that pig! Come on! We Dream Curlys can do anything as long as we stick together! Right, Taylor?

(He tries to recapture the spirit of the opening number.)

SEE THOSE WEENIES AVIATE!
THEY'LL BLAST RIGHT PAST HOG HEAVEN'S GATE!

*(**TAYLOR** exits.)*

WHEN PIGS...

Frank?

*(**FRANK** starts to answer, then chokes. He coughs up a pink feather. He's done.)*

Jacob?

*(**JACOB** turns away.)*

Brian?

BRIAN. Howard, you just go too far. When you decide what you want to do, we'll be in the dressing room.

*(**BRIAN, FRANK,** and **JACOB** start to exit.)*

HOWARD. Wait! Hey, guys – come on!

(A final desperate appeal.)

TAKE A LOOK AND YOU MIGHT SPY
ARNOLD ZIFFEL ZOOMING BY...

*(**FRANK** and **JACOB** exit.)*

WHEN PIGS...

BRIAN. Howard! Can I tell you something? Nobody knows who Arnold Ziffel is anymore!

HOWARD Sure they do! He was that cute little pig on *Green Acres* with Eddie Albert – who was in the movie of *Oklahoma!* with the original Dream Curly, James Mitchell! And he went on to...

BRIAN. Nobody cares! Honey, you need to move on. Do a podcast like everyone else.

(BRIAN *exits.* HOWARD *is left alone.*)

HOWARD. I can't understand it. I could see it all so clearly in my mind... What am I going to do?

(*He sinks to his knees.* MISS ROUNDHOLE *appears.*)

MISS ROUNDHOLE. Have you thought about chicken farming?!

HOWARD. Miss Roundhole! What are you doing here?

MISS ROUNDHOLE. I'm a Guidance Counselor, Howard. You look like you could use some guidance.

HOWARD. Yes, Miss Roundhole.

(MISS ROUNDHOLE *pulls out a five-foot-tall Aptitude Test. Boxes next to her pre-printed recommendations are checked off. Psycho piano chords.*)

MISS ROUNDHOLE. Watch Repair! Garden Supply! Plumbing! Chicken Farming...!

HOWARD. (*Reacting like a vampire to a crucifix.*) No! No! No! Miss Roundhole, why are you doing this to me?

MISS ROUNDHOLE. It's my job, Howard.

HOWARD. But I got rid of you!

MISS ROUNDHOLE. Ha! I'm with you always. Now, let's review. Up till now you've been doing things your way. Where has it gotten you?

HOWARD. I'm broke, my friends won't speak to me, and I'm in the middle of a show with a finale that doesn't work.

MISS ROUNDHOLE. Exactly. The Theater is impractical, Howard. It's too expensive. It's out of date. It doesn't work.

HOWARD. *(A whimper.)* Maybe you're right.

MISS ROUNDHOLE. Of course I'm right! Wait and see; it won't be so bad. Plumbers get to wear funny clothes. Watch Repair can be creative.

> *(***MISS ROUNDHOLE*** *crosses right and peers at him over the top of the Aptitude Test, her fingers drumming on it nervously.)*

HOWARD. *(Unsure.)* I guess it might be...

MISS ROUNDHOLE. Might be what, Howard?

HOWARD. It might be...okay.

MISS ROUNDHOLE. *(Triumphant.)* Yes, Howard! And that's all anyone can expect! Okay is good enough!

> *(Nightmare Psycho piano chords. She laughs maniacally. As she does, her head spins 360 degrees. Note: This is achieved through having a double "be"* **MISS R***'s hands when she goes behind the aptitude test. To simulate the head spin* **TAYLOR** *simply turns around.)*

HOWARD. All right, Miss Roundhole! You win. I'll try every one of those jobs if you just promise to leave me alone!

MISS ROUNDHOLE. *(Emerging from behind the aptitude test.)* You've got a deal!

> *(They shake on it. The deal is sealed. Suddenly* **HOWARD** *has second thoughts.)*

HOWARD. ...But my friends are still waiting backstage – and there's an audience out front. I can't let them down. I've still got to come up with a finale.

MISS ROUNDHOLE. Oh, I see. You're going to take on four new careers and finish your show all at the same time?

HOWARD. I can try. Maybe I can. Do you think so?

MISS ROUNDHOLE. Well, Howard, I'd say there's a chance you might pull it off... WHEN PIGS FLY!

> *(Her last word echoes as she and the aptitude test disappear in a flash of lightning.)*

HOWARD. You wait and see, Miss Roundhole! I'll do it! Somehow... But how...? I'm so confused...

[MUSIC NO. 29 "TARA UNDERSCORE"]

> *(A dramatic light change. As* **HOWARD** *wracks his brain he hears a montage of overlapping voices.)*

JACOB. *(Voice over.)* It' s not that we don't love Howard – he just tends to get a little carried away...

BRIAN. *(Voice over.)* ...You just go too far...

MISS ROUNDHOLE. *(Voice over.)* Okay is good enough...

FRANK. *(Voice over.)* I need a bigger finish...

BRIAN. *(Voice over.)* I told you this wouldn't work...

MISS ROUNDHOLE. *(Voice over.)* Okay is good enough...

OTHER VOICES. *(Voice over.)* The rich red earth of Tara... Tara... Tara.

> *(***HOWARD*** *has picked up the wrong frequency. He shakes his head and gets his channel back.)*

JACOB. *(Voice over.)* What do you want to do, Howard...?

MISS ROUNDHOLE. *(Voice over.)* Watch Repair, Garden Supply, Plumbing, Chicken Farming...

BRIAN. *(Voice over.)* You just go too far...just go too far...
Go too far... Go too far...

OTHER VOICES. *(Voice over, joining in.)* Go too far. Go too
far. Go too far...

HOWARD. Wait!

> *(He gets the Big Idea. With a wave of his arms
> he cuts off the voices. Lights restore.)*

Wait! It's not that I go too far. It's that I haven't gone
far enough...!

> **(HOWARD** *has had a revelation. Now he puts
> it into words, tentatively at first, gaining
> confidence and momentum as he goes.)*

[MUSIC NO. 30 "OVER THE TOP"]

THERE'S A PLACE I'VE DREAMED ABOUT,
LIKE PARADISE BUT FARTHER OUT.
HOW TO GET THERE, WHO CAN SAY?
THERE'S NO MAP TO SHOW THE WAY.
IT'S WAITING SOMEWHERE OFF THE SCALE...
AROUND THE BEND... BEYOND THE PALE...

OVER THE TOP.
I WANNA GO OVER THE TOP.
I'M READY TO PACK UP AND MOVE
TO THE PLACE I CAN PROVE
I DON'T KNOW WHEN TO STOP.
I'M GONNA STAKE MY CLAIM
WHERE IT'S NEVER THE SAME-OLD SAME-OLD
SHOULD I JUST STAY PUT AND PAINT BY NUMBERS?
DON'T INSULT ME!
CATAPULT ME
OVER THE TOP.
I WANNA BE MORE THAN OK.
I WANNA RELOCATE MY BASE

TO THAT MAGICAL PLACE
I CAN GO ALL THE WAY!
I'LL BUILD MY CASTLE IN THE AIR,
AND THAT'S WHERE I'LL SET UP SHOP.
WHEN I'M O-O-O-O-OH
OVER THE TOP!

> *(A hard-edged spot hits* **HOWARD**, *who exudes assurance and showmanship. There's no turning back now. The Austrian drape rises.)*

And now ladies and gentlemen, presenting our grand finale! *When Pigs Fly* would like to remind you that even the most mundane profession can be fabulous! Watch Repair!

> *(The black curtains part, revealing* **FRANK**. *He's costumed in outlandish showgirl glamor as "Watch Repair."* **HOWARD** *presents him in the manner of a Ziegfeld tenor singing "A Pretty Girl is Like a Melody.")*

Garden Supply!

> *(Now* **BRIAN** *appears in a showgirl "Garden Supply" drag.* **HOWARD** *parades him across the stage.)*

Chicken Farming!

> *(***JACOB** *appears as the last word in "Chicken Farming.")*

Plumbing!

> *(***TAYLOR** *completes the picture in a lavish costume salute to "Plumbing.")*

ALL.
TAKE IT O-O-O-O-OH
OVER THE TOP!

HOWARD.

> I'M GONNA FIND THAT SPOT
> WHERE ALL THAT YOU'VE GOT IS ACCEPTED.
> WILL THE COMPROMISERS OVERTAKE ME?
> THEY CAN'T LICK ME!
> JUST DROP-KICK ME
>
> OVER THE TOP.
> I WANNA BE ONE OF A KIND.
> I WANNA CREATE A DISPLAY
> THAT MAKES EV'RYONE SAY
> THAT I'M OUT OF MY MIND!

ALL.

> WHEN YOU GIVE YOUR ALL TO JUST ONE DREAM
> MAKE SURE IT'S THE CREAM OF THE CROP.
> TAKE IT O-O-O-O-OH
> OVER THE TOP!

> *(**HOWARD** exits. One at a time, the **OTHERS** step down for the traditional Zeigfeld showgirl recitation.)*

FRANK. Though cuckoo clock and pocket watch are really rather charming,

The time pieces I tinker with are often more alarming!

> *(A cuckoo pops out of the clock at his crotch.)*

JACOB. It's sad to earn a living supplying poultry buyers.

I start out with these cute young chicks and end up pluckin' fryers!

> *(A fringe of rubber chickens falls from beneath his skirt.)*

TAYLOR. I flush with pride as I display the best in bathroom chic,

And plunge right in to clear your drain or fix that pesky leak!

(He squirts the audience.)

BRIAN. I'm the one you come to when you want a hoe.
I've got ev'ry thing it takes to make a small thing grow!

> *(Green boas are released and flowers pop from flowerpots on his hips.)*

QUARTET.
WHEN YOU GIVE YOUR ALL TO JUST ONE DREAM
MAKE SURE IT'S THE CREAM OF THE CROP.
TAKE IT O-O-O-O-O, O-O-O-O-OH, O-O-O-O-OH...

> *(**HOWARD** re-enters, all in white – the Dreamiest Dream Curly imaginable.)*

HOWARD & ALL.
WHEN PIGS FLY
GRAB YOUR OVER-THE-TOP HAT!
WE'RE DRESSED FOR EXCESS, THE LIMIT'S ONLY THE SKY!
THE SHOW'S A QUEER ONE, THERE'S NO DOUBT:
IT'S NOT ONLY OVER, IT'S OVER AND OUT!
SO AU-RE VOIR, AUF WIEDERSEHEN, GOOD-BYE!

HOWARD.
AND THOUGH OUR FLIGHT OF FANCY'S THROUGH,
REMEMBER THIS: DREAMS DO COME TRUE

ALL.
WHEN PIGS
WHEN PIGS FLY!

> *(Blackout. The finale costumes are seen in silhouette as the stars on **HOWARD**'s costume strobe.)*

> *(Bows. Music continues under. **HOWARD** moves to the edge of the proscenium and turns back to see... The silhouette of a Winged Pig flies across the cyclorama.)*

[MUSIC NO. 30 "FINALE PLAYOFF"]

HOWARD. *(Very Porky Pig.)* Th-Th-Th-Th-That's All Folks!!!

(Blackout, curtain.)

End of Play

www.ingramcontent.com/pod-product-compliance
Lightning Source LLC
Chambersburg PA
CBHW070357120726
47909CB00008B/2892